Rasulka & Taratha

A Mermaids Vengeance

Ken Gardner

Rasulka & Taratha
A Mermaids Vengeance

ISBN: 9798712761180

Author: Ken Gardner

Copyright © 2020

Contents

Dedication

This book is dedicated to my Goddess who has been my muse and inspiration to me throughout writing this book.

Acknowledgement

I would like to acknowledge Grace Williams who has helped me to re-edit my work and for her assistance and patience. I look forward to working with her again on my next book.

Prologue
Late 1979

The last thing John Bachall remembered was following his mark down an alley way towards the cove opening. He had heard whispers of the vampire mermaids that lived amongst the seashells, but he had heard that their sirens song always lulled you into an erotic coma.

The next thing he felt was a slap to awaken him from what he thought was the perfect dream. There she stood, his lover, Rusalka Eveshka, a Mermaid in her human form, a form that he hadn't seen in years.
When he started working as a Federal Employment auditor he was told that he had to be a single male so he left his love and started going undercover to stay on the trail of a criminal gang who stopped paying their Federal Employment Taxes until he was caught in that alleyway and drugged by Rasulka and her friend.
"My love, why are you doing this to me? Why have you drugged me?" John whispered to Rasulka and then froze as another beautiful mermaid approached in her current human form.
"It's him isn't it, that's the man that left you to

the wolves?" her voice hit a pitch that made his body crave to be naked and tied to a bed with both these beautiful women using him as their own personal boy toy as they whipped him and sodomize his body.

"Yes, he is the one that left me at the cove the day, after telling me he was leaving me, the same day that the gang took away our little submissive boy." Rasulka sang in that one voice that plays on repeat in his recurring fantasies.

John watched as both females glided towards the bed that had him strapped spread eagle on a fourposter bed, each female dressed in skintight hot pants and a striped shirt, their Farrah Fawcett hair style bouncing with each step.

Rasulka, ran her sharp finger down his naked form and leaned into whisper,

"Let Taratha and I tell you the story of how your selfish ways, ruined our lives and brought forth the anger that has her and I wanting nothing more than to devour you, and leave you for dead, but first we have been without life substance for a while and need a fill up." She smiled as her teeth elongated as Taratha began to remove her clothing.

They both approached John's tied body and started piercing bites up his legs from his ankles to just below his torso, where his thighs joined his groin, a St. Andrews Cross made of flesh; they sucked his blood from his body leaving him in a euphoric state.

Each time they detached their succulent lips from his body it had him arched in the air, the need to orgasm had become strong. His body was wrought with desire to ejaculate his seed every time the females bit down, but it disappeared when they stopped just short of his throbbing erection.

Rusalka smiled "That shall do us for a little while, now at one time you were Kur, my lover from before the deluge. At the same time you died, Taratha had found and lost Sukarney, her lover. Then, as your soul was reincarnated as John Bachall, Sukarney's soul found a home as Nathanael Levine, descended from Hebrew Priests."
Taratha wiped her mouth and sat naked beside John's head as Rasulka straddled his lap, pushing her smooth, hairless womanhood down his hard, long, thick erection, it slid easily into her. He knew he couldn't hold on for long, it felt like a memory of having her before, she slid up and down him slowly, her fingernails piercing his skin on his already bloody skin. Taratha let out a cry strong, at first almost painful, but then extremely pleasant a hot explosion surged from him his body convulsing as every drop emptied into her leaving him drained of all his strength.

Chapter One
1979

Four AM Saturday morning, the Jewish Sabbath in Salt Creek Heights, Illinois.
As Sam Mendota, turned off the flashing neon lights of his well-established Strip and Clip joint, the street it was located on was heavily taxed by the local criminal syndicate, The Kasbah Club advertising its sexciting all nude Las Vegas revue.

It was April 1979, he wondered how much longer he wanted to look at naked young strippers —shaking their behinds and the multitude of blonde, brunette, and manicured pussies, their legs always smooth for the clientele to run their hands up and down.
It no longer mattered how often the girls bent over and spread their cheeks for the entire world to see their anuses. It no longer thrilled him as it did when he collected the nightly street tax from suburban prostitution cribs, as a tough 19-year-old thug from the Warsaw ghetto for Jake Guzik in 1929.
He drank schnapps, whiskey, and wine to wash away the nightmares of Florida.
Often, he and his all-purpose car parker shared drinks and work together. They were both haunted by the events of Florida. At times they almost convinced themselves it never happened.

Almost.

His old-fashioned sports coat reeked of stale beer, whiskey, bad after shave, and that strange fruity vaginal spray the strippers use to make their pussies taste delectable for the clients.
A fifty-dollar bottle of Champagne, a quiet booth to spend one hundred dollars only to have the girls grind their naked bodies on the male's laps, until they had become so turned on they orgasmed.
As a form of sexual pleasure without penetration, if you paid more to go upstairs, you could experience the full talents of the nude stripper you were with.

He used to hate to see the young females come into the business, but when he saw the track marks on their arms, he insisted they cover them as much as they could and told them not to shoot up in the club. It was still his business and he didn't need it marred by drug addicts who couldn't handle their drugs.

He had just turned sixty-nine, and if it wasn't for his second wife, a non-Jewish woman, and his two sons from his second marriage, along with his High school senior daughter, paying the IRS and having his attorneys on call, he would have been ready to retire to Palm Springs, where his arthritis wouldn't hurt so much. He was 5ft 7 with stooped shoulders and prostate that made peeing a misery from Gehenna, the Jewish hell.

He paid Oliver Bascomb, the black doorman, sometime hitman, bouncer, a retainer in cash, one hundred dollars, who would park the cars, crack heads, and could smell trouble from some customer or a bad underage punk with a bad Driver's License. Oliver thanked him and left in his rusted ten year old Cadillac, (good cover for the cops) after telling him that one of his main money makers, Rasulka Eveshka and her lesbian girlfriend Taratha Moksoh were in their own Lincoln Town Car (good investment Sam told them) in the lot behind the club wanting to talk to him.

Rasulka was about twenty-five, with a great shape and long dirty blonde tresses she always had pinned back. She said that she was a White Russian, born in Macao. Her extremely statuesque figure drove all the men and a handful of women crazy. All she had to do was flash her pussy and its natural blonde pubic hair that was neatly trimmed into the shape of a fish she would have the stage littered with cash.
She learned to dance in the Far East, with an extremely seductive swaying of her hips, like a cobra dancing to an Indian faker's flute, hypnotic siren like moves. Her breasts were large and her hips wide in the perfect curve and legs built

strong, like a long-distance runner. He always pictured what he would do if his daughter ever walked in, a daughter from his first marriage she was a swimmer and developed strong arms and a similar figure. She had married only showing up after she had his grandchildren.

When Rasulka pushed six-dollar cocktails, she was almost never turned down. One regular said that she had the perfect action when giving a blow job and always swallowed the release.
She knew the art of giving a man enough that would make him have multiple erections, effectively draining him, as his second orgasm flowed through his body.

He had hired her friend, Taratha, as a part-time dancer, who had an almost identical figure but had even longer scarlet tresses. He had heard that she also worked for Tony Spitz, in one of his massage parlors, The Sultan's Delight. She was the parlor's Dominatrix, as Mistress Katrina. Her scarlet bush was also trimmed into the form of a fish or a dolphin.

He saw their car and walked across the icy parking lot towards them.
As Rasulka rolled down the window she pointed "Get in the back seat."
She wanted to increase Taratha's hours. She used her thumb to guide him to the back. Once

inside, he saw that Taratha was wearing a raincoat, unbuttoned enough to reveal that she was topless, possibly nude. She sat smiling like a flirting teenager, on bent, raincoat covered knees.

Rasulka turned on the overhead light. Rasulka seldom smiled, carrying herself like a Queen when she spoke, but tonight she sounded happy.

"Taratha has developed a new act. She wants to show you."

Taratha pulled off her raincoat slowly and seductively, Sam had expected she was naked. As she lifted her coat from under her, he saw that she was wearing a costume, something tight, grey and from her bellybutton down, accentuated the fine curve of her long legs; it looked like the bottom half of a strange evening gown, but it was so tight her thighs were pushed together.

As it tapered down to her legs revealing a large flat fantail like the dolphins he had seen in marine shows. On either side of her thighs, were small airplane-like wings or fins, when she bent over to unbutton his fly, he noticed a larger dolphin like dorsal fin between her shoulder blades. He had seen things like that deep-sea fishing in the Caribbean and the Atlantic. He had heard about mermaid striptease shows in Vegas. He wondered if she wanted to start one here, at the Kasbah Club.

Shaking his head, "I don't think we can invest in a large enough tank for a Mer..." he gasped as he saw Taratha's sharp shark-like row of teeth. Taratha had pulled down both his pants and boxers, revealing an erection he never imagined he would achieve again. Rasulka had positioned herself around him from the front seat. She licked his ear, pushing his old-fashioned fedora over his eyes. He couldn't move, as she tilted her head slightly kissing his mouth and down his neck.

"Sam, I can't say that this is only business. This is personal too, this is for our enabler Nathanael Levine, whom you helped kill back in Florida."

She bit down on his neck and he moaned and screamed out as the pain from the bite mixed with the pleasure from the situation he was in. His euphoric orgasm sprang forth so quickly that he started to fall asleep. Just as the second bite from Taratha broke the skin into his inner thigh, making his erection throb with the need to chase the pleasure his body was feeling. As his life passed away, he ejaculated. Taratha feasted on his seed, wiping her face noisily as she finished.

Chapter Two

As was his habit, Oliver Bascomb drove his 1970 rusted out Caddy down Roosevelt Road, searching for young tail for a blow job. As he approached, the intersection of Pulaski Road and Roosevelt, a mocha coloured hooker motioned for him to pull over into a mostly hidden alley.

Before he knew it another young dark-skinned girl in hot pants and white knee-high boots joined them in his newspaper, cigarette butt, and empty Styrofoam cup filled backseat.

The mocha skinned girl then tapped him on his shoulder as he turned she pushed her tongue, deep into his throat. As he was forced to accept her tongue his body was pushed against the now locked driver's side door as his erection was gripped tight in a soft female hand. As the tongue in his mouth turned him on, the hand on his cock jerked quickly.

He could hear a British accented voice which sounded like Taratha's, giggling girlish voice.

"This is nothing personal Ollie-lay. This is business. We can't have a witness, my love."

He had remembered sending Sam to the rear of the Kasbah Club. As Taratha's voice gave an exaggerated sigh, he noticed the mocha female had changed into Rasulka and her teeth were sharp like a great white.

He felt his belt being pulled from his pants as Taratha forced his hands above his head tying them with the belt and hooking them to the bar over his head.

He closed his eyes briefly before opening them seeing the scarlet haired Taratha licking his now erect uncircumcised manhood, using her lips to pull back the foreskin so she could run her tongue across the now exposed sensitive head.

He moaned as his eyes fell shut. The image of the beautiful Taratha's tongue touching his head made his hips buck up as she started smiling and giggling, the last words he heard before he felt Rasulka move down from his mouth to his neck, were from Taratha:

"Grandma, what big teeth you have!"

His last sensation was the orgasm that had him filling Taratha's mouth with his seed, a euphoric feeling from his release.

Chapter Three

"I have the POA, you know the Power of Attorney for the Kasbah Club and I will appoint a younger, tougher thug or a strong arm to manage that poontang palace.

"You're my attorney, Sidney. Tell the press that we support the Police and any help we can offer the Sheriff's department on who slaughtered those two dumb bastards, we will."

Joseph "King of Bohemia" Warsawsky, a nickname given to him by some Police reporter from the city news bureau a few decades ago, slammed down the phone. The mutilated bodies of Sam and Oliver had been found in Salt Creek Height's face down in the sand of Oak Street Beach.

The Times, The Tribune, and all the local West Suburban Press were on the prowl for new or more information. There were rumors that the victims were killed by some new Charles Manson style gang. A gang obsessed on erasing the syndicate right from the top down.

He had been the one to identify the bodies, his long life as the control of the city's sin street tax collection and everything that he had seen are what prevented him from vomiting, as the officers took him to the morgue to identify the butchered, pale, and anemic corpses.

He shifted his weight in his chair, the thought of Sam and Oliver's bodies lying on the cold slab, brought vomit to his throat. He dialed Bernard Bacalovaky, a longtime collector of the sin street tax department to protect the clubs, massage parlors, and BDSM dungeons. When Bernard picked up his phone, he was at his favorite porn theater which served as his headquarters.
Warsawsky spoke with the voice of a man granting a kingdom to rule. "Bernie, you are now the Emperor of your own place now, the Kasbah Club is yours, at last."

Chapter Four

I am John Bachall, a Federal Unemployment Tax Enforcement Agent. The sovereign states are not to be trusted with the disbursement of the Unemployment Insurance benefits.

I guess you could say we are the political thugs, investigating whichever party is not in power and its members within the national crime syndicate.

That's how I imagined it happened in Salt Creek Heights, after Warsawsky gave his orders.

As everyone knows he was only one cog in a major outfit. His crew oversaw the management of places that provided sexual pleasure to members of the opposite or same sex for affection or meet a social contact to administer more exotic passions, those places which the outfit did not own.

They collected a street tax, which provided protection for the independent operators to stay in business. It was also well known that Warsawsky advocated the sub-contracting out of those services to independent operators. Letting them deal with the overhead and the management of the property and employees while the criminal gang, known as The outfit supplied the legal muscle to provide protection from those in the two political parties and the smaller suburban parties.

He preferred to deal and dine with those in power. For those independents that did cooperate, taxes would always be collected from them with assistance of firearms or, in most cases, a beating or two.
This made the independent operators keep two or even three sets of books, one for them, one for the outfit, and one for the various village, township, county, state and with the Federal taxing agencies, it did not matter if the source of the income was legal or not.

Uncle Sam demanded his share with the help of Auditors, like me. I work for a special oversight agency within the Executive branch known as Section 2600, we are charged with the enforcement of overseeing who was an employee and who was not. The people who were not considered by their employers to be an employee under Section 2600 received a 1099 at the end of the year and were required to make quarterly payments, they are withholding in their various income, social security, and Medicare taxes. We have less than 100 employees, only one half of which was SPAIFs, Special Agents in the Field, of which I am one of, the rest are accountants, attorneys, and political appointees relating information to the President. It's an easy job; we are trained to fire guns, but never use them. A 38 revolver mixed with boxing, judo, and whatever else the government hired from a political contributor were used to train us.

The sources of information mostly comes from anonymous attorneys, CPAs, accountants, bookkeepers, and the unemployed, who could not be paid for the unemployment insurance benefits all with a personal political axe to sharpen.

Rasulka and Taratha entered my life because of a fired female bartender, Carla Hofmeyer, who was also a pimp on the side, she didn't get her two weeks separation pay and decided to call the agency to come and collect. It must also be noted that all three are descendants of Adam's first wife, Queen Lilith, and Fallen Angels, Nephilim. They are shape shifting immortals, which can only be killed by silver stakes into their hearts. They were also blessed with incredibly hypnotic singing voices, an unbelievable beauty; they become seductive sirens right out of Homer's Odyssey, resembling mermaids.

When they seek out sexual pleasures from their mates, they are like Black Widow spiders, desiring your XY chromosome in your sperm and blood to stay alive.

If they love you and do not want to kill you, then you must become their slave, subject to the pleasure form of torture, in order for them to suppress their desire to have you, for a meal.

Thier lover is Enoch, Son of Cain, the killer of Adam's second son, Abel. They are members of the Cult of Atargati, their Ruler, known as Queen Lilith; Queen Lilith is the first of the pre-deluge world.

When she was the ruler of her kingdom, the Creator sent in a giant comet to the sea, to destroy mankind by flooding and other comets, fire, meteors, brimstone, rain and all the un-moored debris of the solar system; thus resulting in fireworks known to the survivors, with its flaming aurora borealis, lighting, showering the world with rain. As chunks of shrapnel began to fall from of the sky this became known for several millennia as the Night of the Comets.

Chapter Five

It was on the evening of October 30, 1978, when the opening of the Cult of Atargati war against mankind, the Blood Wars, began.

Since no woman could be harmed as they are immune with the XX Chromosome, the Blood Wars began, not with a bang, but with a splash of water from a dolphin like mammal in the Gulf of Mexico.

On a sandy island located south of Naples, Florida, once used by rum runners in the 1920's, still used by drug and rum smugglers in 1978 to land their drugs and booze from Jamaica and Central America.

As it is now known to all with the opening of portals to other alternative worlds, Prohibition was never repealed in this blood war, violence drenched world.

The attempts to pass repeal of prohibition amendment have failed because the national crime syndicate or the Outfit, along with the politicians that support, was making too much money by keeping booze illegal. The Amendment, though in effect, also helped the efforts of the Cult of the Atargati who felt booze poisoned the male breeding stock and XY Chromosomes.

After their evening swim, Rasulka and Taratha without transforming their twisting tails into legs, embraced and kissed, enjoying the way each other's skin felt against their own.
In their mermaid form, they massaged the smoothest part of their fantail; this was the hidden area where they could enjoy being connected with a human male and stimulate their clitorises until reaching orgasm. They touched, licked and nibbled at each other's most sensitive body parts driving themselves into a euphoric pleasure filled release.

Once they had come down from their orgasmic tryst and enjoyed a burst of endorphins the grew tired as they crawled under an abandoned Seminole Tiki hut for privacy.
The heat generated from their sensual love making, kept them warm since Southwest Florida in the fall turns cool in the evening with cool breezes blowing in from the Gulf of Mexico.
They were still in their Atargati mermaid form when a Diamond- backed rattlesnake slithered out and towards Taratha.
The scarlet haired Taratha, still enjoyed playing with snakes after several thousand millennia, she allowed the four-foot reptile to slither over her body as it searched for heat, exploring first between her breasts, then around her neck. Taratha imagined what a wonderful souvenir

necklace it would make.

Rasulka glanced over with boredom in her eyes. She knew Taratha was childlike, cruel, easily bored, and as frightened as she was when they first met. They had no mothers since theirs were both killed when the Supreme one got bored with the Earth and decided to destroy it. As the Diamondback got bored it turned and rattled its tail in Taratha's face. Taratha struck, by opening her mouth full of razor-sharp teeth biting the rattle off in one chomp. Startled the Diamond struck back at her with her venom filled fangs biting her scaled thigh. Taratha twisted her six-foot tail around the wounded serpent as she squeezed, but before the serpent would die, Taratha severed the head. Once the snake was dead, Taratha decided it would not make a nice necklace and tossed it away, as a human would a banana peel or apple core.

Rasulka changed back to her human form, her tail shrinking from seven feet to her normal human size of five foot eight inches. Taratha changed to her human form, like Rasulka, she was as naked as the day a human was born, neither moved for a few moments, but as always after any blood is shed, whether a reptile or a human male, they hugged, as if in remorse.

The snake provided no nourishment or ended

the desire for the blood or semen of a human male; they hugged, sharing the heat of each other's body before gently placing their lips together, exchanging a seductive kiss.

Rasulka, broke the silence first, "You know a snake cannot kill us, when we are in the form of Astargoti, and you continue to do that when you know you are just being mean to things that have to follow their instinct just as we have to follow ours."

Taratha, pretended to pout, and then smiled. "I know that, but it's fun to fool them—just as we fool our prey in order to eat." She laughed as she licked her lips.

Rasulka shook her head "No."

Taratha started combing the sand out of Rusalka's long blonde hair with her fingers, stopping only to sniff and kiss a few strands of her waist long blonde hair.

Rasulka continued: "The last time I spoke with some of Lilith's Atargati Elite Agents, I was told that she hired a human scientist to try to find the cure and rid us of the need to drink the blood of human males."

Taratha laughed into the wind, "It would be fun to have male enablers—our very own slaves to bring other human males into our harem to use, instead of us dressing to entice them. After all, humans use dogs to hunt prey for them—maybe it is meant for us to have tried our own human male dogs again. We have not used any for at least a century and a half or so." Taratha's hazel eyes widened as she thought of the hunt.

"I do not agree, even if we are as naked as we are now,"—she raised her eyebrows in feign embarrassment---"we should never be naked to danger, whether we are in Astargoti form of a Mermaid, a Werewolf, or a Bat. We should never let our defenses down. We should only be human to attract prey or to what the humans call fuck so that we may have children for a short time before they mature and leave us after a few months." Rasulka tried to make her words sound final.

Taratha laughed as another breeze blew in, another serpent slithered near, a smaller coral snake. She picked it up and drained it until it shriveled into a fraction of its former size.

They didn't fear any of Florida's snakes since evolution long ago gave them immunity from poisonous reptiles and insects.

Taratha stood up and looked at the sky. Rasulka followed her gaze. They both saw a shooting star, Taratha whispered to Rasulka, "It's time to go, the rain is moving in quickly."

Rasulka stood up; brushing away the particles of sand, as she hugged Taratha's shivering body. "There's no rain—no sign of it anywhere." She whispered before she licked Taratha's right earlobe, placing her sharp teeth against the lobe.

"What about that star?" Taratha's moaned response had Rasulka smiling. "That star wasn't rain—it was just a---", Rasulka licked her neck.
"The night the comets fell—first there was a star, then some rain, fire, brimstone then one comet after another, then the rain---" Rasulka bit down on her sensitive skin.
"There's no sign of---" Taratha started shaking and then Rasulka, kneeled, slowly pulling Taratha down, as Rasulka cradled her whispering a rhythmic pre-Sumerian song that her own lost mother used to sing to her. In those two months when they were leaving pre-adolescence into young womanhood, on many, many nights before the comets fell and the rain flooded the Tigris and Euphrates flood plain.
It was the same song her mother, Ejdera, sang to her that night that caused Taratha to shiver every time she saw a shooting star race across a cloudless night. Rasulka also remembered that there were no clouds the night the comets fell and the rains flooded the land.

They instinctively uncoiled their tails for protection in case they needed to suddenly hide in the Gulf until the danger they sensed passed them. A truly nude mermaid is one in naked human form if caught by surprise before they change into something else.

Chapter Six

In the early morning, hidden by yet another abandoned Tiki hut, Ex-Sargent of the US army Rangers, Nathaneal Levine, a former resident of Salt Creek Height's Jewish Ghetto called the Viet Nam veteran had watched the two Mermaids make love for fifteen minutes.

His nose filled with cocaine, as he pulled out his erection, which he thought was dead from the war. He grew hard until he overcame his guilt of watching the sensual love making, his need of self-pleasure arose as he gripped his erection in his hand, stroking himself slowly up and down his length, the image of the two beautiful creatures licking and sucking each other, had him chasing his orgasm in minutes.

He put down his pint of Cuban rum, feeling so many emotions run through him.

"Who are these women?" he whispered to himself.

Did he imagine them to be Mermaids since Holloween began at midnight, maybe they were lesbian flappers, similar to the shows he had seen in Paris, Thailand, and Hong Kong practicing an act to separate lonely men from their money.

He took another gulp. He wanted to join them,

he felt a trance invading his mind, as he wanted to be the man to serve them, protect them, to make love to them.

He didn't want to be lonely and he didn't want to drink himself into impotence anymore.

Nathaneal moved closer and listened, making sure that he didn't encounter any snakes. Rasulka and Tartha spoke in a mixture of a British and vaguely American, almost Salt Creek Heights Yiddish/Italian accents.

He continued to listen to them talking, what he considered girl talk, the strange high pitch song they sang, made his body crave another release. They sounded like college radicals, who he had met at various meetings around the USA for Jewish war vets.

He drank some more, but now he wondered not who they were—but what they were? Where did they come from?

As they spoke, the blonde combed out the auburn hair of the other, only stopping to exchange kisses and massage her breasts until her nipples were peeked and hard, he felt his erection growing once more.

Who were these women and what kind of powers did they possess? Nathaneal decided to do as he always did when encountering females, he decided to go over and introduce himself to the blonde and auburn, in hopes that the females would allow him to give them the pleasure they were seeking.

Chapter Seven

Not that far away in Seminole Sy's Alligator Wrestling and Farm, between North of Goodland, several miles south of Naples just off of the Tamiami Trail, Edwin Maxwell of the Chicago's Northside Narcotics crew leaned back in the Seminole's rocking chair, thumbing through the latest copy of a Supermarket newspaper Tabloid.

His left hand holding a Rum N Coke and the other holding the magazine open, he was reading about strange human creatures that had been spotted roaming the Everglades by Park Rangers. Some reported finding the mutilated corpses of Florididian natives and Seminoles in Mangrove swamps, drained of blood and in some cases, castrated.

As Maxwell read on he felt a twinge of pain pass through his gentiles as he instinctively uncrossed his legs and patted the revolver on the table next to him. He placed the magazine in his lap and yelled out to the Seminole who was gutting a baby gator for a taxidermy job.

Have you ever heard of gators or people being found mutilated in the mangrove swamp?" He quoted the passage. "I want to know so I can get in the Halloween spirit for the tourist broads."

Sy turned and sat down, resting his folded arms on the back of the chair. After he cleaned his hands with an old blood-stained towel, he adjusted his straw Stetson so the band could absorb any perspiration on his forehead. Then he re-lit his pipe and replied stoically:

"A few times. The killers just left partially skinned, gutted corpses of their victims; some have figured that they were just drunken poachers who got killed when they passed out from too much bad brew, or going where they shouldn't be going. None of my people though. We know better than to go wandering around the glades unless we know where we are going. I strip them of anything valuable and let the glades take care of them."

Maxwell laughed. "Sy you're as cold blooded as those Redskins outside the doors of old time cigar stores. Were they drained of blood?"

Sy squinted for a moment and spoke: "I didn't give it much thought and come to think of it, some were missing their balls and cock, with their pants completely removed, probably thought they were getting oral pleasure, but were being nibbled on by the gator they couldn't kill. It's funny, but the wind always sounded like the laughter of a girl or a woman, that's right a woman's laughter at her own private joke."

"Is that why you don't poach at night?"

Sy didn't say a word as he got up and split the gut of another gator to be stuffed for a tourist.

On the opposite side of the table was his foot-long Gig, a three-pronged trident used for spearing fish and small alligators. Each of the pyramid shaped tips were filed sharp enough to pierce a gladiator's shield.

Chapter Eight

Nathaneal glanced down at the dead Diamondback and the shrunken coral snake, glanced back for a moment, then decided against leaving, trying instead to introduce himself to the buxom beauties.

He smiled at them, wishing he wasn't so scrawny. He felt himself becoming aroused by the sight of the women and knew that his ragged khakis could not hide the bulge.

"Hello, I am Nathaneal Levine, I'm from Salt Lake Creek, it's the second biggest city in the good old US of A," he smiled at them before speaking again "I never saw anything like yous in my life. Those are the most realistic Halloween costumes I have ever seen."

Taratha's hypnotic, high pitched song and gaze caught his eye, as she began to take control of him.

Rasulka, did nothing, since she knew that the week or two gap in their ages made Taratha a younger, more immature in thought Atargoti woman, but also a very aggressive predator. They both needed nourishment. However, she didn't want to push Taratha. If she wanted an enabler to be their slave, or if she just wanted someone to be their meal.

Taratha started to transform, and as her tail faded to legs, Rasulka started. In their black Ford they had their clothes, but they were more relaxed remaining nude.

Taratha and Rasulka remembered the pleasure of the Hebrew King Solomon's harem and Taratha wanted to examine their prize catch. After she commanded the mesmerized Nathaneal to strip, Taratha, remembered her days as a disguised male Nurse in the Union Army, during the American Civil War. Where she had cured the wounded, she still maintained her maternal nursing instincts and to feed on those who passed away. Her eyes began to examine Nathaneal's swollen member, tucked snugly behind his pants.

Chapter Nine

Rasulka was about to join Taratha when she heard some splashing behind them. She turned to see Seminole Sy stepping out of the nearby Mangrove Swamp, the morning sun interfering with a scene he didn't expect to find when he went poaching on Federal land.

Although the women were nude, he vaguely remembered their features as belonging to two sharply dressed college girl types who stopped by his Alligator Farm to admire a rare-caged Crocodile that was caught in a nearby bayou. They bought some fresh everglade garfish filets which they rapidly consumed raw before he could wrap them in paper.

Rasulka didn't bother to cover her nakedness and let her human teeth change to fangs as did Taratha, who began to change her legs into her a longer than usual tail.
Taratha's face remained beautiful as she lowered herself to ground and began to silently crawl towards Sy. He began to step back into the Mangrove Swamp up to his knees, failing to notice that Rasulka, in spite of her growing feeling that being predators was wrong, assumed the same form and slid silently into the water behind him, her tail propelling her

towards his legs without causing a ripple.

The need to survive propelled him forward, hurtling the Gig at Taratha, the trident striking deep into her shoulder, causing a small squirt of scarlet blood to shoot out of her sternum, the hole being an insult to her scar less feminine skin caused her to strike while Rasulka did the same. Rasulka pulled Sy underwater with her tail while Taratha pulled out the trident. Soon her skin began to heal as she was in her non-human form.

Sy was dragged up on the beach and stripped naked. He was so frightened from the creature's that were now attacking him that he emptied his bowels. Yet, he was so turned on by the scene that he had walked up on that his manhood swelled into a steel erection.

The women's bites sent pleasure roaring through his body as his orgasm was ripped from his loins in an explosion, as if he was undergoing a self-pleasure ritual.

Being close, Rasulka let her companion enjoy her favorite part of the male anatomy, as Taratha enjoyed her coral snake earlier.

No matter how many books they had read in the centuries since Gutenberg printed books, no matter how many artists and philosophers they had known, they remained predators.

Not fearing reptilian predators, still in their

Mermaid forms, they dragged Sy's remains as far out to sea as they could where they hoped the featureless body would appear to be another victim of some unknown creature of the sea.

Back on the beach, they resumed their human forms. After a large meal, they relaxed and slept. After waking up from a peaceful sleep they decided to wake Nathanael from his trance like state. Their need to feed heightened at the sight of his engorged manhood they decided to relieve him of his semen through oral pleasure. As they licked and bit at his body, his need to touch them grew and he began running his finger over their sensual places, seeking out the feel of the women that were now bouncing on his lap. They decided that once they detoxified him permanently, he could be trained to be a good enabler slave. They allowed him to dress since they were done with him. They watched over him while he rested.

Taratha realized instinctively, that he was her Bronze Age lover from Deluge, who died in the last battle of mankind.

Chapter Ten

Edwin Maxwell was pissed, at around Seven o'clock. he began to wonder about Seminole Sy's absence. He was at least an hour late. They had a load to pick up from Jamaica from Goodland Island. He was getting really angry with him, he began pacing.

Edwin went from being a WW2 Irish immigrant, union strike breaker and became a great union organizer for the building industry. When someone had pointed out the benefits of having Union dues paid by the workers, not to mention the various health, welfare, pension and other funds that were paid by the employers on behalf of the workers.

The building contractors could only use unionized labor on government projects. He now lived on Salt Creek Heights' Gold Coast and was a major benefactor of the Parish. He was no fool, when he moved into his blue blood apartment building, which he knew before hand to restrict the residence to non-Catholics, he modified his brogue to Presbyterian Scotch. With his lease in hand, placed a bright green Shamrock by his apartment in the same location that a Jew would nail his Mezuza.

For a drug delivery of this size, he needed someone to handle the boat. If Seminole Sy didn't show up, he would be forced to use the two crackhead friends of Sy's, Cappy Isaac Coffin, for the cabin cruiser, and James Belmonti, his first and only mate.

He motioned Raymond Bloch, his second in command and the one he considered his most dangerous gunman, to get out of Sy's rocking chair. Bloch was one of the last of Lake County Illinois slot machine kings. Maxwell, found out it was safer to pay tribute, a percentage of his sales, to the outfit. He didn't need the cash for himself, but to support other vice operations on the North Side. Whatever he could chisel from his smuggling operations, would stay his unless someone got stoned and spoke loosely to those outside his crew.

Only those assembled knew about this and his future smuggling plans. Maxwell looked at who was here: Leo "Lumpy", Cohen, Leo Schtarker, Anthony Felice, John "Lucky", Godard, Charles McClane, and John Blaine; all gunman and assassins who enforced the verbal contracts with the few thousand speakeasies they were allowed to conduct transactions.

He lit a Cuban cigar, blowing a few smoke rings while staring at the ceiling, calculating costs and profit from this operation. He wished he was back in Chicago, enjoying the memories of the private burlesque Halloween show, of undressed dirty blond showgirls pleasuring themselves with the tips of broomsticks or grinding down on the floor. God almighty, he hated Florida, but after tonight, he still had to go on his treasure hunting trip for pirate's gold on Goodland Island.

Maxwell leaned his rocking chair forward, turning to Raymond, "Screw Sy, he's out of this deal. Find that local moonshiner Florida natives. We have our appointment tonight."
The door opened, and in walked the outfit's representative, Sam Mendota, from the Kasbah Club, asking for the nearest toilet.

Chapter Eleven

As Maxwell and his gang loaded into two black Caddys and one truck to go and meet Captain Coffin and his one-man crew. They were observed with numerous notations on yellow legal pad by one of the Treasury Department's best IRS Agents, Sandra Merrow, and her subordinate agent, Scotch accented Ben Varrey. Unknown to the US Government, Sandra Merrow was aided in her ability to fight US Income Tax evaders. Powers she had acquired centuries ago by being a member of the Atargoti. She received incredibly loyal help by her enabler or slave from Scotland, Ben. Her official assignment was to track down and arrest the Chicago labor leader known as Edwin Maxwell. Her unofficial one was to track down and convince wayward Atargotis to return to the Atargati race in order to continue their plans to civilize and maintain a steady source of human males to increase their numbers.

After Ben started the Ford to pursue the gang, Special Agent Merrow opened a thermos bottle and poured a cup of blood taken from a corpse of a former male stockbroker who stopped to ask directions to Fort Meyers Beach. She was happy to relieve the stockbroker's neck stress with a massage which was due to the Wall Street

Crash of 1978, which had occurred the previous week.

Sam Mendota had arrived with Oliver Bascombe. Sam decided not to coordinate the Gang himself. He decided to put Edwin in charge to make arrangements with Cappy and James for the boat; they had an arrangement with Edwin, to make the pickup out beyond the 12-mile marker with a small fast freighter.

Chapter Twelve

As if time had stood still, Nathaneal, Rasulka, and Taratha had formed a sort of Garden of Eden, a naked paradise.

Using some ancient incantations, they are able to replenish and heal Nathaneal's health, drying out his booze, and drug addictions. He was mesmerized by their history, as Taratha told him that he descended from her pre-deluge lover, Sukarney, and that she intended to use gold from the treasure they have found to nurse him back to health, protect him, he became her male enabler. Even Rasulka, had warmed to him, she and Taratha decide to make him their enabler. At this point Sam Bachall was to be found later as he was investigating The Outfit's failure to pay their Section 2600 taxes in Salt Creek Heights.

As they approached the coral reef where their treasures of the centuries were hidden, Rasulka sensed that there was something wrong in the Gulf of Mexico. She saw the small gang near their coral reefs.

Rasulka and Taratha gathered their accumulated treasures from wrecked galleons.

Ben Verrey knew that there was more beneath this reef, in order to, draw them out, he started spinning a tale to the third generation Irish Gangster hit men, about the Scots having power of prediction.

Ben convinced Edwin to go ashore to the reef to find the gold doubloons, which were more and more valuable since double digit inflation began with the 1973 and 1979 oil shock to the USA's economy.
He played upon Maxwell's fears of another great depression since the huge stock market crash Maxwell ordered the freighter to stop as the crew disembarked for treasure.

Rasulka explained to Taratha their treasure was in danger, they both decided to do something about it. They figured that Nathaneal was safe, when they left him, armed with their tridents, to go out to the sea as mermaids, to protect their treasure.

Using the power of the Tridents to raise the water, the reef began to get covered by the water.
One by one, they pulled the gangsters and crew under; taking their time to build up a whirlpool under the water to jam the propellers. As the men approached the reef, they saw the rising sea level, as they tried to swim away, Rasulka and Taratha, revered to their Bronze Age warrior siren mode. Via their siren's seductive pitch,

they seduced them with song. Rasulka and Taratha stripped them of weapons and clothes. They drained them of their virility, of their seed, blood and life force with undersea oral pleasure. They sank, their flesh fading, their skeletons dissolving.

Rasulka and Taratha were stronger, with the extra nourishment; they climbed on the deck to confront Ben Verry. Still in his sailor form, he warned them in his sly brogue, not to attempt any tricks on him. He explained that he and Sandra Merrow were sent on a mission by Queen Lilith to bring back all of the errant Atargatis' to her palace on an Aegean Island. He explained in his persuasive manner that Queen Lilith must bring back all of the Atargati, to replenish the cult, saying that new spirits in human form with powers and long hidden tribes out of Asia were going to try to battle the Christians, the Muslims, Hindus, and the Jews. Queen Lilith foresaw a global war in the future.

Rasulka listened to what he had to say. When she had heard enough, she informed him that she could destroy him, if she found out he was lying.
He told them that their new enabler will not survive another night if they do not return. He named John Bachall as the reincarnated lover of Rasulka and he was in danger of being killed by

Queen Lilith's gangster enablers back in Salt Creek Heights. The two errant Atargati jumped back in the water racing through a now violent storm, courtesy of Queen, Lilith back to Nathaneal.

Ben, using an incantation, guided the empty ship back to port, running it aground at a beach North of Naples.

Ben disappeared and the remains of the freighter became another Marie Celeste mystery of the sea. Using telepathy, he communicated to Sandra in her old woman disguise.

Chapter Thirteen

Once they heard of the abandoned freighter, Sam, Oliver and all the others trudge through the tropical growth looking for Seminole Sy, believing that he was drunk somewhere.
Out of the growth, Sandra, in disguise as a now alluring female shaman, dressed in a flowing black gown, her hair long and dark parted down the middle like a dominatrix. Presenting a smoke enveloped performance, she informed them that their freighter was attacked by demons of the sea. She drew a large hexagon in the sand and in the middle, a vision of mermaids devouring the gangster crew. She warned them that a merman lays in wait for them ahead in a clearing and to not be fooled by his human form. She warned them that merfolk walk on land and must be killed before they end their criminal empire. She faded away, into the night as quickly as she arrived.

As if on cue, the ground beneath John turned into quicksand as he was swallowed; his skin became covered in leeches. This spooked the remaining gangsters. They began rushing towards the clearing to save themselves.

In the gulf Rasulka and Taratha fought swarms of fish and entangling, flesh eating seaweed, entrapping them, slowing them as they fought the sea from trying to seize their tridents.

The remaining gangsters fought the tropical overgrowth. Without machetes, the jungle seemed to take on a life of its own.

An unnamed Seminole Indian guide was grabbed and smothered by a huge leafy tree, with growing tendrils killing him by strangulation. Sam started muttering the Jewish Prayer, the "Shema."

When they reached the clearing, the last Seminole guide fell to his knees and prayed.

Rasulka and Taratha, reached the shore, their tails refusing to retract stopping theie legs from forming. They lay on the shore looking at the sky and saw the face of Queen Lilith smiling before she disappeared behind the clouds. They were forced by the Queens power to crawl through the jungle, their almost bare bodies, and gorgeous blue and silver tails, now bloodied filled with cuts and gouges.

Chapter Fourteen

The gangsters confronted the naked Nathaneal, as Sam muttered, "A merman?".
The gangsters circled him, as the Seminole guide stood off to the side, it was now very dark except for the light of the campfire. As they drw their pistols and revolvers, a standoff, waiting for Nathaneal.

Still in their mermaid form, Rasulka and Taratha were held back by the vise like grips of cactus plants that had crept up through the earth. They could see Nathaneal, naked and defending them, but the face of Queen Lilith kept flashing in front of their faces, drawing a finger over her lips, preventing them from speaking.

Each one of the gangsters whispered, he is a merman, but neither of them fired a shot.
The face of the Queen appeared over Nathaneal as Sam screamed, "DYBBUK!"
They all began to fire, obliterating the body of Nathaneal. Their shots piercing his skin, blood spewing from the wounds, his body lay lifeless.
The gangsters fled one by one behind the Seminole. A flaming will of the wisp, gliding them back to their cars,
The bloodied legs of Rusalka and Taratha came back, as they memorized the faces of the killers,

the cactus plants sank back into the ground as Taratha started to shiver and tears welled in her eyes. Taratha cradled the bloody remains of Nathaneal. Rasulka stared at the retreating outlines of the gangsters. She heard the ghostly laughter of Queen Lilith in the breeze.

Chapter Fifteen

In Washington, the images appeared to John Bachall, at first in a dream and then in nightmares. The siren like figure of his Rasulka appeared in all her nude glory moving closer to him, as he reached out to touch her his manhood hard and weeping for her he woke, he rubbed his eyes realizing he was in his room. It had all been another dream.

In my asylum's room, I spend my days dreaming of my Rasulka, unsure if the golden mirror I stole from her in that Salt Creek Heights Dungeon was real, or if it was something found in a treasure hunt.
And I have a dream:
Around eight o'clock, Rasulka awoke and found Taratha cradling the naked Nathanael stroking his hair and sniffing his unshaven face. She had made a campfire and smiled at Rasulka, her fangs reverted to human form. "He will make a good enabler, he's like a pet, a dog!"

In the glow of the fire Taratha's hair turned a brighter scarlet. Rusalka, felt a little jealous of the attention paid to Nathanael by Taratha. Then she noticed Nathanael's manhood harden and she moved towards them, wanting them both. She snapped her fingers and they woke from their embrace. Rasulka wanted to forget the violence of the day. Predators must protect and make love to her cubs, even one she knew was once a lover in days passed.

The End

Thank you.

Thank you for joining me on the short journey of
Rusalka I hope you enjoyed it.
Look out for my next book which is a collection
of Mermaid stories.

About the Author

Ken lives in Chicago USA. He has been writing short stories since the 1980's having been published in many top shelf magazines and he wanted to write about his passion of mermaids. He enjoys entertaining people with his work and is fascinated by the supernatural
This is the first book of many.

He admires Authors like Edgar Rice Burroughs, HP, Lovecraft, Ray Bradbury, Stephen King and the classic detective and mystery authors.

Facebook www.facebook.com/author.ken.10